Fat Witch Rides Again

D1464192

Also by Margaret Ryan

Fat Witch Rides Again
King Tubbitum and the Little Cook★
King Tubbitum at the Fair★
King Tubbitum and the Great
Spring Clean★
Queen Bea the Champion★
Queen Bea on Holiday★
Queen Bea's Christmas
The Secret of the H.C. Factor

★*Available from Mammoth*

MARGARET RYAN

Fat Witch Rides Again

Illustrated by Emma Chichester Clark

MAMMOTH

EAST LOTHIAN
DISTRICT LIBRARY

WITHDRAWN

JF
5

First published in Great Britain 1990
by Methuen Children's Books Ltd
Published 1991 by Mammoth
an imprint of Mandarin Paperbacks
Michelin House, 81 Fulham Road, London SW3 6RB

Mandarin is an imprint of the Octopus Publishing Group,
a division of Reed International Books Ltd

Text copyright © 1990 Margaret Ryan
Illustrations copyright © 1990 Emma Chichester Clark

ISBN 0 7497 0722 4

A CIP catalogue record for this title
is available from the British Library

Printed in Great Britain
by Cox & Wyman Ltd, Reading, Berkshire

This paperback is sold subject to the condition
that it shall not, by way of trade or otherwise,
be lent, resold, hired out, or otherwise circulated
without the publisher's prior consent in any form
of binding or cover other than that in which
it is published and without a similar condition
including this condition being imposed
on the subsequent purchaser.

Contents

CHAPTER ONE

New Brooms for Old

Fat Witch juddered down from the sky on her broomstick and parked it outside Mrs Copper's cake shop. She pressed her green nose against the shop window and tried to decide which cake to have with her morning coffee.

'Should I have the chocolate gateau, or the lemon meringue pie?' she wondered. 'That raspberry sponge looks nice too. And the strawberry cheesecake. Oh, I can't decide.'

So she went inside the shop and bought them all. When she came out she said, 'Sorry I was so long, broomstick. But I nearly fell over Small Witch in there. I had to lift her up so that she could see over the counter. She was buying the TINIEST fairy cakes. Hardly a bite in them.'

Then she loaded the four boxes of cakes on to the broomstick.

'Creak,' said the broomstick.

Then Fat Witch got on.

'Creak and double creak,' moaned the broomstick.

'Shush,' said Fat Witch. 'It's only a little shopping. Take me to the supermarket.'

The broomstick jolted into the air, dithered over the rooftops and, with a sigh of relief, deposited Fat Witch at the supermarket.

'Now wait in the car park,' said Fat Witch. 'I won't be long. I just want to get something for my tea.'

An hour later Fat Witch appeared pushing a trolley containing four carrier-bags.

'There were so many tasty things,' she said to the broomstick, 'that I just couldn't decide. But luckily I met Tall Witch inside and she reached lots of nice things for me that were on the high shelves. And I bought a nice tin of polish for you. It's your favourite Dark Tan.' Then she loaded the four bags on to the broomstick.

'Creak,' said the broomstick.

Then Fat Witch got on.

'Creak and treble creak,' moaned the broomstick.

'Shush,' said Fat Witch. 'It's only a little more shopping. Take me to the sweet shop.'

The broomstick heaved itself into the air, flopped around the chimney pots, then dumped Fat Witch at the sweet shop.

'I won't be a moment,' said Fat Witch as the broomstick lay gasping on the pavement. 'I just want to get some jelly babies, then we can go home and you can have a rest. Poor thing, you do seem tired today.'

It was a long time before she came back.

'Sorry I was such an age,' she said. 'I met Granny Witch in there buying her wine gums and she stopped to have a chat. But I got the jelly babies and some caramels, some fruit gums and some peppermints, and some ice-cream. So we'd better hurry home before it melts.'

She loaded all the bags of sweets on to the broomstick.

'Creak,' said the broomstick.

Then Fat Witch got on.

'Double, treble and a zillion creaks,' gasped the broomstick.

'Shush,' said Fat Witch. 'A few jelly babies can't be that heavy. Take me home now.'

The broomstick did a funny little hop and threw itself into the sky. It hovered there for a moment, just over the childrens' play park, then, with a final 'CREEEAAAK' it tilted to one side and tipped Fat Witch and all her shopping into the village duck pond.

'Ow, ow, ow,' yelled Fat Witch, as she floated among the lily pads with lemon meringue pie and ice-cream dripping down her nose and a very surprised frog clinging to her pointed hat.

'Quack, quack, quack,' said the ducks as they nibbled daintily on the unexpected feast of soggy chocolate gateau.

'What did you do that for, broomstick?' asked Fat Witch, trying to rescue her shopping as she waded out of the pond.

But the broomstick, which now lay gasping on the grass, was too exhausted to speak.

'Oh, dear,' said Fat Witch. 'You don't look at all well, broomstick. I'm really sorry I worked you so

hard. I'll carry you to the garage for repair.'

She gathered up the rest of her shopping which had floated to the edge of the pond, cradled the broomstick under her arm and hurried to Big Al's garage.

Big Al was in the garage forecourt polishing windscreens on his second-hand cars when she arrived.

He shook his head when he saw the broomstick.

'You've done it now, Fat Witch,' he said. 'Just look at this machine. It's worn out. How am I supposed to repair it? I warned you last time you brought it in that it wouldn't hold your weight for much longer. Now you'll have to trade it in for something a bit sturdier. How about a long-handled scrubbing brush? That should hold you nicely, and it's very reliable.'

'But very dull,' said Fat Witch. 'Not a lot of style.'

'All right,' said Big Al. 'If you don't fancy that, how about this deck brush? It's second-hand, but a good-looking model. Came from a royal yacht, you know. Last owners were very particular. It does tend to roll a bit when cornering. But if you drive carefully . . .'

But Fat Witch wasn't listening. She'd got her eye on a sleek sporty broomstick lounging just inside the garage door. Its shaft glinted like gold in the sunlight, and its stiff bristles were russet tipped.

'Oh, I like that, Al,' breathed Fat Witch, going over to it and running a hand along its smooth surface.

'Can I have a test fly on that?'

Big Al sucked in his jaws, and shook his head. 'Oh, I don't think that's for you, Fat Witch. Bit out of your price range. It's the very latest model. I only took delivery of it today. Called a "Vroomstick", you know. Very very fast. Streaks across the sky, nippy at cornering, stops dead on the magic word "STOP". Seat-belt and parachute included of course.'

'Of course,' said Fat Witch. 'I'll take it. Can I fly it home now?'

'Hey, wait. Not so fast,' said Big Al. 'Think carefully. Can you afford it?' And he told Fat Witch the price.

Fat Witch's mouth fell open and her ears wound round in circles.

'That much?' she said. 'Even if I trade in my old broomstick?'

'Especially if you trade in your old broomstick,' said Big Al.

Sadly, Fat Witch picked up her old broomstick. 'Come on,' she said. 'We'll go home and I'll find you a nice thick rug to lie on by the fire. Thanks anyway, Al.' And she trailed home. When she got there her cat, Joe King, was sunning himself on the front porch. He opened one lazy eye and looked at her.

'I don't believe my eye,' he said. 'Fat Witch walking? It must be a dream or a mirage or a miracle.'

'My broomstick's broken,' said Fat Witch, and she told him all that had happened.

Joe King laughed when he heard. 'I'm sorry I missed your great splashdown in the duck pond,' he said. 'But, you on a vroomstick? You must be joking!'

'No, you're Joe King,' said Fat Witch.

'Listen,' said Joe King, 'I do the funnies. But where did you think you were going to get the money to buy a machine like that?'

'I suppose I could always try to magic some money.'

Joe King shook his head. 'You know that Chief Witch has forbidden you to do any more magic until you can get the magic rhymes right. Anyway, since when did Big Al take money with "Bank of

Witch Town" written on it?'

Fat Witch looked glum. Then she had an idea. 'Maybe Chief Witch would lend me some money,' she said. 'I'll fly – er – walk over to see her right now.'

She left Joe King to work on his sun-tan and set off at a brisk pace.

Chief Witch lived on the other side of the village and was just sitting down to her lunch when Fat Witch arrived. Fat Witch explained all about the old broomstick and about the cost of the new vroomstick. 'And I just wondered if you might lend me the money to buy it?' she finished, standing on one leg and keeping her fingers and eyes crossed.

'Neither a borrower nor a lender be,' said Chief Witch looking stern.

'Does that mean yes?' asked Fat Witch hopefully.

'No,' said Chief Witch.

Then Fat Witch looked so unhappy that Chief Witch softened a little and said, 'But I was going to send for you anyway, Fat Witch. There is a very

important job to be done that could EARN you the money to buy the vroomstick.'

'Anything,' said Fat Witch. 'I'll do anything.'

'The job will be dangerous,' said Chief Witch. 'You must consider it carefully. It will need courage. It will need bravery. It may even need the magic of SPECIAL CUSTARD POWDER. I have named it OPERATION CLEAN SWEEP. Now listen carefully . . .'

CHAPTER TWO
Operation Clean Sweep

Fat Witch was all ears.

'I wish you wouldn't do that,' said Chief Witch.

'Sorry,' muttered Fat Witch. 'It just happens.' As quickly as they'd come all the extra ears disappeared from her dress and hat, and left only her normal two which just twitched.

'Do you remember,' said Chief Witch, 'a distant cousin of mine, not far enough removed, called Elf Azard?'

Fat Witch nodded. 'Horrible nasty character with suspicious eyes and a mean look. No resemblance, of course.'

'That's him,' said Chief Witch. 'Well, I've just had word from Witches' headquarters that he's up to his old tricks again and is roaming the countryside making mischief and mess wherever he can. In the next town he stole one of the bin lorries and emptied its contents in the middle of the town square. And now it seems he's arrived here. Have you seen the village green this morning?'

Fat Witch shook her head. 'Has it been stolen too?'

'Covered in Chinese takeaway cartons,' said Chief Witch. 'The handiwork of Elf Azard. And as if that wasn't enough, he filled all the daffodil trumpets with special fried rice.'

'What a waste,' said Fat Witch. 'I'm very fond of special fried rice.'

'The problem is,' said Chief Witch, 'that he's never forgiven me for taking away all his magic powers because he used them to harm people. But he can be just as nasty without them. I want him caught before he does any more damage. And that's where you come in, Fat Witch.'

'Me?'

'Yes. So far no ordinary person's been able to catch Elf Azard in the act. He's far too clever. But he'd never suspect YOU were after him. So if you can catch him, you will collect the reward I am offering.'

'Well, I'd like the reward, of course,' said Fat

Witch. 'But catch Elf Azard . . . I don't know. Couldn't one of the other witches do it?'

'No,' said Chief Witch. 'Granny Witch is too old, Tall Witch is too noticeable, Small Witch would get trodden on, and Slinky Witch is . . . too . . . unsuitable. You're the one for the job. I know that once you set your mind to something, you really go after it.'

'Well, I would like the reward. But . . . Elf Azard. He's nasty.'

'Think of the vroomstick,' said Chief Witch. 'Think of whizzing across the sky. Think of people saying "Is it a boat? Is it a plane? No it's Super Witch."'

Fat Witch thought. 'I'll do it. I'll do it,' she cried.

'When do I start?'

'Tonight,' said Chief Witch. 'Once it gets dark, hide behind the silver birch tree on the village green. No, on second thoughts, better make it the large oak. Watch what happens. I think Elf Azard may reappear there. He can't resist Chinese takeaways. But remember, only use the magic of special custard powder as a last dessert . . . er . . . resort.'

Fat Witch skipped home, the tip of her tall hat quivering with her news. She was so excited that she didn't notice Joe King asleep on the porch and she tripped over him and landed with a thud on the doormat.

'You have just disturbed a perfectly good dream,' muttered Joe King. 'Why don't you look where you're going?'

'Have I got news?' chattered Fat Witch, not listening to him. 'Have I got news?'

'Well have you or haven't you?' asked Joe King.

'Come inside and I'll tell you,' said Fat Witch. 'It's top secret.'

'I know what it is. Tesco's hamburgers are half price again so you can eat twice as many.'

Fat Witch ignored him. 'I,' she said, 'am going on a dangerous mission.'

'Oh, yes? Walking to Mrs Copper's cake shop and not using the pelican crossing?' Joe King put on his bored expression till he heard what it was all about.

'You're crazy. You're mad. You're bananas. Or possibly all four . . . er . . . three. Operation Clean Sweep. Huh. Operation Clean Off Your Head, more like. Elf Azard will eat you up and spit you out in little pieces. He'll leave YOU littered on the village green. Everybody's afraid of him. Even me. Especially me. What is Chief Witch thinking about, sending you to do this? Too scared to do it herself, I bet. You won't come back alive, Fat Witch. You may not come back at all.'

'But,' said Fat Witch. 'I haven't told you everything.' She lowered her voice to a whisper. 'Chief Witch thinks I'm the best witch for the job, and I'm allowed to take some SPECIAL CUSTARD POWDER.'

'Well,' said Joe King, not convinced. 'You've still got to get close enough to sprinkle some on Elf Azard for that to work. I don't like it, but, I suppose I'd better go along with you and lend a paw.'

'Thank you, Joe King,' said Fat Witch. 'I knew I could rely on you. Now what should I wear to go on this dangerous mission?'

Joe King looked at her. 'I would suggest, since it will be night time, that your long black dress and pointed hat will be excellent camouflage.'

'What about my face?'

'No time for a face lift. Try some soot.'

'Right. What about you?'

'I'm a black cat already.'

'Right. But where am I going to keep the special custard powder? It has to be in a safe place.'

'Under your hat.'

'Great idea. Oh, I'm so excited, Joe King. I wish tonight would hurry up and come so that I can catch Elf Azard and get Operation Clean Sweep over with.'

When night did come, Fat Witch and Joe King crept along the village street and hid themselves behind the oak tree on the village green, just opposite Mr Wong's Chinese Takeaway.

It was a good evening for business. Lots of people came and bought their food and carried it home in the square containers. There was Mr Gristle the butcher, whose favourite dish was Pekin duck. There was the Reverend J. Moneystone, who

was very partial to sweet and sour pork, and the honourable Mrs Amanda Pale-Brown Hatt whose rabbit pie had run away and nearly ruined her dinner party till she remembered about dear Mr Wong's special Prawn Surprise which was made with haddock. But they all hurried home with their purchases and didn't spill a drop.

It got later and later. Fat Witch got colder and colder. And Joe King got crosser and crosser.

'I could have been curled up at home watching the telly,' he muttered. 'I've already missed the nine o'clock mews. I bet Elf Azard's not going to appear.'

'Maybe he's turned over a new leaf,' said Fat Witch hopefully. 'Or maybe he's heard that I'm after him and he's too scared to come out.'

'Don't be ridiculous,' snorted Joe King.

Just at that moment there was a loud crash as a shadowy figure appeared and kicked over a litter bin. It went rolling along the ground, scattering its contents far and wide. A dull thud followed as the shadowy figure tipped up a park bench flattening a bed of flowering tulips. Finally there was a clatter of tin cans as the shadowy figure booted them into the air, scoring imaginary goals.

'He's here,' whispered Fat Witch.

'Wish I wasn't,' muttered Joe King.

Elf Azard came swaggering across the village green, red tights tucked into his green boots and his red and green tunic covered in yesterday's dinner. He peered round about him then went into Mr Wong's Chinese restaurant. He strode up to the counter. 'Six chicken chow mein and six special fried rice,' he snarled to Mr Wong. 'And make it snappy. I'm hungry.'

Mr Wong wrote down the order and hurried away to get it. He knew that while Elf Azard was in the shop his regular customers would stay away.

Meanwhile Elf Azard nosed around, anxious to find more mischief to get up to while he was waiting. He spied something on the counter. 'Aha, paper napkins,' he muttered. 'Just the thing.' And he picked up a pile, shredded them into thin strips and scattered them all over the shop. Then he noticed Mr Wong's fish tank with several Angel fish swimming peacefully among the greenery. 'Feeding time, boys.' he grinned nastily, as he emptied a bowl of prawn crackers in beside them. The fish dived for cover as the bowl came in as well. Finally, he emptied out the daffodils from the vase on the counter and pulled off all the petals one by one.

Fat Witch scowled when she saw this. Chief Witch was right, it really was time Elf Azard was taught a lesson.

Then Mr Wong appeared with the order and before he got a chance to say anything about the mess, Elf Azard bounced out of the shop and parked himself on the village green to eat his food. Off came the tops of the food boxes and these were tossed on the grass. Then Elf Azard gnawed his way though all the chicken legs and threw the bones into the bushes. After that, not two metres away from Fat Witch's sooty nose, Elf Azard began to fill the trumpets of the daffodils with special fried rice.

It was too much for Fat Witch. She loved daffodils and special fried rice, but not together. Without thinking, she leapt out on Elf Azard and grabbed him by the arm. 'Got you, you menace,' she shouted. 'I'm going to turn you in.'

Elf Azard looked up in surprise.

'Why, if it isn't Fat Witch,' he said. 'And her

idiot cat.' And he brushed Fat Witch off his arm and Joe King off his leg as though they had been fleas.

'So you think you're going to turn me in, do you? Now there's a good joke. Ha, ha, ha. I just can't stop laughing. But I'll have a joke on you, Fat Witch. Let's have your pointed hat. I've always fancied myself in one of these. How would I look as Witch Azard?' Then he pulled off Fat Witch's hat and saw, strapped to her head, the packet of special custard powder.

'Aha, what have we here? Custard powder? I bet it's not. I bet it's witch's gold. I'll have some of that.'

'Don't touch it. Don't open it. You don't know what it can do,' cried Fat Witch, but it was too late. Elf Azard had opened the packet and rubbed a pinch of special custard powder between his finger

31

and thumb.

BANG!

He disappeared immediately and in his place stood a rather surprised red and green mouse which Joe King pounced upon and held carefully in his mouth.

Fat Witch picked up the packet of special custard powder, closed it carefully and put it back under her hat.

'Well, he certainly saved me the trouble of sprinkling some on him,' she said to Joe King. 'Let's get him to the police station as fast as we can.'

They hurried along the village street, not talking at all in case Joe King dropped his squeaky mouthful, and they arrived, breathless, at the police station. The police station was part of Constable Goggin's house, and there was a delicious smell of bacon and eggs, Constable Goggin's favourite snack, coming from the open kitchen window. Constable Goggin could be seen inside, his trouser legs rolled up to his knees and his size sixteen feet soaking in two basins of soothing hot water. He splashed to the door when Fat Witch and Joe King rang the bell.

'Well done,' he said when Fat Witch told him all that had happened. 'I knew it would take a bit of magic to catch that one. He was a bit too slippery for me. But don't you worry. Now that I've got him, I'll lock him up good and tight.'

'He'll change back to himself again in about an hour and be none the worse,' said Fat Witch. 'Meanwhile, what Joe King and I need is some sleep. We want to be up bright and early in the morning to collect the reward from Chief Witch.'

Fat Witch went home and dreamt of zooming across the sky on her new Vroomstick. Joe King went home and went to sleep. It had been a tiring sort of day.

Next morning Fat Witch and Joe King hurried along to Chief Witch's house.

'I can't get used to this walking business,' Fat Witch said to Joe King as they set off. 'The sooner I get that new Vroomstick the better.'

Chief Witch was sitting at her desk looking grim

34

when Fat Witch and Joe King went in.

Fat Witch didn't seem to notice. 'Well, I did it,' she chirped. 'I captured Elf Azard single-handed, and double-pawed, and now I've come to claim the reward.'

'Reward,' said Chief Witch. 'There is no reward. There is no Elf Azard. Elf Azard has escaped.'

'Escaped,' gasped Fat Witch. 'But how?'

'That daft policeman locked him in a cell while he was still a mouse,' said Chief Witch. 'Elf Azard simply sneaked out through the bars when Constable Goggin wasn't looking.'

'Oh, no,' said Fat Witch.

'Oh, yes,' said Chief Witch. 'And now he's being an even bigger menace. After he escaped last night and changed back to himself, he went out and tied toilet rolls to all the dogs in the area, and let them run loose. The countryside is now covered in pink toilet paper. He's made more mess than ever. He's got to be stopped, Fat Witch. Once and for all.'

CHAPTER THREE

Smelly Elf Azard

Fat Witch trailed home with Joe King at her heels. Over a cup of tea and a sticky bun they discussed the problem.

'What we need to do,' said Fat Witch, 'is to try to think like Elf Azard. To put ourselves into his boots, and decide what he's going to do next. Perhaps that way we can catch him.'

'Great idea,' said Joe King. 'But how do we do that? Buy up all the blue toilet rolls in the shops?'

'Don't be silly. Elf Azard's out to make as much mess as he can so he'll be looking for ways to do that. Let's have a look in the local paper and see what's happening round about. That might give us a clue as to what mischief he might get up to next.'

They searched through the paper.

'Butter's up two pence a pound,' said Fat Witch.

'Two firemen had a blazing row,' said Joe King.

'Wait a minute, look at this, Joe King. It says here that at noon today Mr Horseborough, the mayor, is to open a new perfume factory on the outskirts of the village. I just bet Elf Azard would love to mess that up. I think we should be there just in case. Come on, if we hurry we can get there and find a hiding place before the ceremony begins.'

'But you've no broomstick,' Joe King reminded her.

'There's a bicycle in the coal shed,' said Fat Witch. 'We'll go on that.'

The bicycle was very old and very rusty.

'I hope no one I know sees me travelling on this,' said Joe King. 'This is not my kind of transport. I have my image to think of, you know.'

'Shush and get on,' said Fat Witch.

Soon, with Joe King crouched low in the

shopping basket on the front, they were on their way, squeaking and clanking down the road.

'Is this supposed to be a secret mission, Fat Witch?' asked Joe King. 'Because if it is, we're not exactly being stealthy and quiet. We can be heard for miles around.'

'Double bluff,' panted Fat Witch. 'Since we're making so much noise, no one will suspect we're on a secret mission. If Elf Azard is there, he'll think we've just come to see the opening. He's bound to be fooled.'

'Oh, yes?' said Joe King. 'Wake me when we get there.' And he curled up into a ball and went to sleep.

Meanwhile Fat Witch whistled a tune in the key of U.R. flat as though she hadn't a care in the world. She looked all round as if searching for a good picnic spot, but really she was keeping a sharp look out for Elf Azard. After a few wrong turnings and teeth loosening bumps they arrived at the factory. Fat Witch pulled hard on the brakes and stopped so suddenly that Joe King was almost catapulted out of the basket.

'Where am I? Is it morning? I want my breakfast,' he said.

'Shush,' said Fat Witch, parking the bicycle behind a tree. 'I think the opening ceremony is about to begin. The mayor is sitting over yonder on that high platform. That woman beside him must be Madame Kennelle, the famous perfumier and the factory owner. It said in the paper she'd be here. But there's no sign of Elf Azard. Maybe he's hiding, maybe he's not coming, maybe we guessed wrong.'

Just then, the mayor stood up to begin his

40

speech. He gave a polite little cough behind his hand.

'Ahem, ahem. Ladies and Gentlemen,' he said. 'Today it gives me great pleasure to declare open this beautiful perfume factory. I know that Madame Kennelle has worked very hard to create the most beautiful smells imaginable . . .'

At that moment, Fat Witch's nose began to twitch, Joe King's nose began to quiver, and Madame Kennelle's large hooked nose almost

wrinkled back into her face, for coming out of the factory chimney was the most foul, most horrible, pongiest smell ever. Everyone coughed and spluttered and held hankies to their noses, but Fat Witch just muttered, 'Elf Azard.' She jumped back on to the ancient bike and began pedalling as fast as she could towards the large chimney.

'Hey, wait for me,' shouted Joe King as he took a flying leap on to her shoulder. He missed, and clung on to her back, spreadeagled like a miniature black tigerskin rug. Reaching the small door at the base of the chimney, Fat Witch leapt off the bike. She threw open the door and rushed inside. There

was Elf Azard all right, standing barefoot beside the factory furnace, and burning a pile of his smelliest red tights.

'Of all the barefooted cheek,' said Fat Witch. 'But I'll get you this time, Elf Azard.' And she reached under her hat for the special custard powder.

At that moment, a very loud voice from behind shouted. 'I demand to know the meaning of all this.'

Startled, Fat Witch turned round. So did the custard powder which scattered all over Mr Horseborough, the mayor.

BANG!

He immediately changed into a donkey.

Fat Witch was horrified and said, 'Oh, no.'

Elf Azard was delighted. 'Maybe we should team up, Fat Witch. I could let you do my dirty work for me. Be seeing you.' And he pulled on his boots and was off like the wind.

The mayor, meanwhile, looked rather surprised and said, 'Hee Haw.'

Fat Witch didn't wait to explain what had happened but led the donkey to her bike and, finding a piece of old string in the saddle-bag, tied him to the handlebars.

With Joe King sitting on the donkey's back she led them all back to the Town Hall.

'Put this donkey in the mayor's room,' she told the astonished Town Hall clerk. 'The mayor will be back soon.'

Chief Witch was none too pleased when Fat Witch reported to her what had happened.

'Changing the mayor into a donkey is not the smartest thing you've ever done, Fat Witch,' she

said. 'And you're no nearer catching Elf Azard. Perhaps you'd better forget all about buying the vroomstick and buy a walking stick instead.'

CHAPTER FOUR

Operation Cobweb

But Fat Witch was still determined to get the reward. She went into Big Al's garage to have another look at the vroomstick. It stood in the corner, gleaming, its beautiful light oak shaft, satin smooth. Fat Witch looked at it and sighed. She could just picture herself up there in the clouds, vrooming past all the other models and graciously waving to passers by. She practised a little gracious wave and clonked Big Al, who had just come up behind her, on the nose.

'Oh, sorry, Al,' said Fat Witch. 'I didn't see you there. I was thinking about the vroomstick.'

'Id's doe use, Fad Widch,' said Big Al, holding his nose. 'You'll never cadch Elf Azard and claim the reward. Thad's twice he's escaped. He's doo smard for you.'

'Too smart, is he?' said Fat Witch, annoyed. 'I'll

show you who's too smart. I'll catch that villain if it's the last thing I do.'

And she stomped past Big Al and out through the garage doors. It was a pity she was too annoyed to notice the patch of oil on the garage forecourt. It was a great pity she'd never been good on slides. WHEEEEE. It was an even greater pity that the car wash was being tested just then. WHOOOOOSH. But it was fortunate that there was a large pile of old car tyres on the far side of the car wash for her to crash land on.

'AAAAAAAH'

Big Al shook his head.

'Her head's in the clouds,' he muttered. 'What a pity the rest of her is lying on the ground.'

But Fat Witch wasn't to be put off. By the time she'd walked home she'd dried off and had a plan.

'Wake up. Wake up, Joe King,' she said, clearing both him and her knitting off the kitchen table with one swipe. 'I've got a plan.'

'And I've got a broken leg,' said Joe King, giving
a realistic limp across the floor. 'I wish you
wouldn't do that. If you want me off the table, you
only have to ask. Nicely. Three days in advance. In
writing.'

'Look,' said Fat Witch, 'I'm sorry I moved you
from the table, but be sensible. I need your help. I
also need the table to write on.'

She got out a large piece of paper and wrote PLAN at the top.

Joe King peered over her shoulder.

'I like it so far,' he said.

Then she wrote OPERATION COBWEB.

'I get it,' said Joe King. 'Out go the clean sweeps and in come the big friendly spiders. We ask them to knit us a giant cobweb, and then we creep up on Elf Azard, throw it over him GOTCHA and claim the reward. Brilliant. Why didn't I think of that? When did you learn to speak Spider, Fat Witch?'

'Don't be three kinds of a dozy-headed cat, Joe King. I asked you to be sensible. The plan has nothing to do with cobwebs except that I'm going to act like a spider and lure Elf Azard into my trap. Now do you see?'

'As well as a blindfolded cat on a dark night,' said Joe King. 'But tell me more.'

'Well,' said Fat Witch. 'We'll put an advert in the

paper, advertising an event that Elf Azard won't be able to resist. That way we'll get him to come to us.'

Joe King put his head on one side and considered.

'No creeping about in the dead of night?' he asked.

'Nope.'

'No more squeaking about on old bikes?'

'Nope.'

'Just sitting about waiting for the bad guy to come to the good guys?'

'Yep.'

'Superb. So what event do we advertise?'

'A fishing competition.'

'A fishing competition? But you know I hate fish. Fish is yuk. Fish tastes . . . fishy.'

'You, are a very strange cat,' said Fat Witch. 'But that's part of the plan. Everybody for miles around knows you can't stand fish, so Elf Azard will never suspect that we have anything to do with it. Get it?'

But Joe King didn't answer. He had already rolled on to his back and thrown his paws into the

air in four gestures of despair.

The following day Fat Witch put an advert in the local paper right beside Big Al's notice announcing the arrival of the vroomstick. Fat Witch's advert said:

GRAND FISHING CONTEST TO BE HELD
TOMORROW. FANTASTIC PRIZE
FOR PERSON WHO LANDS THE LARGEST
FISH. ENTRANTS TO BE BY THE
BIG ROCK ON THE RIVER AT 9.00 A.M.

Joe King, who had recovered slightly by this time, read it and shook his head.

'What fantastic prize are you offering? I hope it's not my *Cool Cats in Concert* album,' he said, clutching it to him.

'Actually,' said Fat Witch, 'I thought I'd try to magic something up for the prize.'

'Oh, no,' said Joe King. 'You know Chief Witch has forbidden you to do any more magic spells until your rhyming improves. Remember last year when you played the Wicked Queen in the Christmas pantomime? You said "Mirror, mirror on the wall, who is the fairest of them . . . please?"'

'I was only being polite,' said Fat Witch.

'And look what happened that Sunday morning when the shops were shut and you tried to magic up a boiled egg for yourself. "Hickerty Pickerty my black hen, she lays eggs for . . . my breakfast." We had enough feathers to fill a dozen duvets and not an egg in sight.'

'That was just a little mistake,' said Fat Witch. 'It didn't seem right to say "gentlemen" when I'm a lady. Anyway I haven't said what the prize is yet, just in case something unexpected turns up.'

Just then, something unexpected did. There was a loud popping noise and Slinky Witch stood skinnily before them. Her long glossy black hair was piled up high on her head and held by two half moon combs. Her turquoise eye make-up matched perfectly the colour of her eyes, and her witch's dress was a designer model. Fat Witch didn't like her much.

'I popped in,' purred Slinky Witch, 'because I've just heard the most ridiculous rumour – that Chief Witch is offering YOU a reward for the capture of Elf Azard. It's not true, of course, is it?'

'Well . . .' said Fat Witch. 'It's really supposed to be a secret . . .'

'You mean it is true! Why on earth did Chief Witch ask you to do it? Everyone knows I would be far more suitable.'

'Chief Witch didn't think so,' said Joe King.

'Quiet, cat,' snapped Slinky Witch, giving him a look that melted his *Cool Cats in Concert* album. 'You haven't heard the last of this, Fat Witch. Not by a long way.' And with another loud pop, she was gone.

CHAPTER FIVE

Fat Witch Does a Spell

Fat Witch and Joe King went down to the river early next morning, and hid themselves behind the large rock.

'Are you sure this will work, Fat Witch?' yawned Joe King.

'Positive,' said Fat Witch. 'Elf Azard is about to learn that he will have to be up early in the morning to outsmart me.'

'There's no sign of him,' said Joe King. 'Maybe his alarm didn't go off. Maybe he's left the country. Maybe this is a crazy idea.'

'Shush,' said Fat Witch. 'Somebody's coming.'

She peered over the top of the rock, but it was only the postman on his way to deliver the letters.

'Morning, Fat Witch,' he said. 'You're up early. Decided to sit outside for a spell?'

'Ha, ha,' muttered Joe King, who settled down

to try to sleep.

Five minutes later, Fat Witch heard a clanking noise, and peered over the top of the rock again. But it was only the milkman on his way to deliver the milk.

'Morning, Fat Witch,' he said. 'You're up early. There must be magic in the air.'

'Everyone's a comedian this morning,' muttered Joe King, still trying to get to sleep.

At that moment a large van rolled up. On the side of it, it said Sid's Fish and Chips. It stopped beside the large rock and just as Fat Witch peered

over, it blared out the most terrible deafening music.

'OH, MY DARLING, OH, MY DARLING OH, MY DARLING, CLEMENTINE.'

'Ow, ow, owl,' howled Joe King, covering his ears with his paws.

Fat Witch pulled her hat down over her ears and strode over to the van.

'What DO you think you're doing?' she said to the man sitting in the driver's seat.

The man turned round. He wore a long white coat and had a white hat pulled low across his face.

'Pardon,' he said.

'WHAT DO YOU THINK YOU'RE DOING?' shouted Fat Witch.

'CAN'T HEAR YOU,' the man shouted back.

'TURN THAT NOISE OFF, YOU'LL FRIGHTEN THE FISH,' yelled Fat Witch.

'What fish would you like?' asked the man. 'I've got plaice and chips, cod and chips and haddock in a curry sauce.'

'I don't want any fish. I want you to turn off that row,' croaked Fat Witch, who was by now nearly hoarse.

But the man just smiled and turned the music up even louder.

'THOU ART LOST AND GONE FOREVER DREADFUL SORRY, CLEMENTINE!'

Fat Witch stomped back to Joe King who was, by this time, trying to stuff his paws into his ears to keep out the noise.

'This is Elf Azard's doing,' said Fat Witch. 'I'm sure of it. He's sent that van here to frighten away the fish, and ruin the competition. Well, he's not going to get away with it. I don't care what you say, Joe King. I'm going to do . . . a spell.'

'Oh, no,' said Joe King. 'Not a spell. You know Chief Witch has told you not to do spells, Fat Witch. You know what happened when you fancied fish and chips for your tea and the fish shop was closed early. Remember, the fishmonger was going to the Fishmonger's Federation Annual Fish and Chip high tea.'

'Well, how was I to know the fishmonger was having his bath when I magicked him up?' said Fat Witch. 'I only wanted him to open up the shop and give me a nice bit of lemon sole.'

'He nearly gave you the sole of his boot. Or he would have if he'd been wearing any. But he did throw his rubber duck at you, didn't he? Trouble is your spells are too unpredictable because of your rotten rhymes.'

'I don't care,' said Fat Witch. 'I'm not letting Elf Azard get away with it.' And she closed her eyes, and began to chant:

'THIS MAN IN A VAN WITH HIS MUSIC
    FROM A CAN
IS FRIGHTENING THE POOR LITTLE
    FISH.
SO TAKE HIM AWAY FOR THE DAY,
    FARAWAY
IS THE MAGIC LITTLE SPELL I . . . MAKE.'

There was a pop, a squeak and a gurgle, and the van disappeared.

'There,' said Fat Witch triumphantly. 'Nothing to it. What did I tell you?'

But Joe King waited and worried. Then there

was another pop, squeak and gurgle, and there appeared along the bank of the river a magnificent orchestra in full evening dress, tuning up in readiness to play. Suddenly the musicians stopped what they were doing and looked round them. They seemed very surprised to find themselves beside a gently flowing stream and began to chatter excitedly in a strange language.

What they said sounded like, 'VOT ARE VE DOINK HERE? VE ARE NOT LIKINK IT. VE VANT OUR MUMMIES.'

'Time to tiptoe away and forget about the fishing competition, Fat Witch,' whispered Joe King. 'No real fisherman would turn up anyway with that racket going on. Elf Azard's been too smart for you again. He must have guessed there was something fishy about that advert.'

Next day, Fat Witch was summoned to Chief Witch's house.

'There is a headline in today's paper, Fat Witch,' she said, 'about a missing orchestra which mysteriously turned up beside our river when it was supposed to be playing at a concert on the other side of the world. There is another item about a fish and chip van which was found on the concert stage where the orchestra should have been. The van was playing "Oh, My Darling, Clementine" very loudly, and the audience were not happy with the switch, so they shouted very rude words at the van driver . . .' and she checked the paper before going on . . . 'the van driver, who was wearing a white coat and hat and green boots. Do you happen to know anything about this?'

Fat Witch swallowed hard and studied the pattern on Chief Witch's wallpaper.

'Because if you do,' went on Chief Witch, 'I may have to consider removing your magic powers as well.'

CHAPTER SIX

Elf Azard's Dirty Tricks

Before Fat Witch could reply, the telephone rang. Chief Witch answered it. 'Chief Witch's residence. Chief Witch speaking,' she said. Fat Witch put on her I'm-not-really-listening-to-your-conversation expression, and pretended to admire a particularly ugly photo of Chief Witch which was hanging on the wall. Unfortunately all the extra ears decided to appear all over Fat Witch's dress and hat and gave her away.

'You can stop pretending you're not listening, Fat Witch,' said Chief Witch. 'This concerns you, anyway.'

The extra ears disappeared and Fat Witch's normal ears twitched in alarm and her hat nearly fell off when she heard the rest of the telephone message.

For his next trick, Elf Azard had broken into Big

Al's garage and had stolen all the cans of paint that
were kept for respraying the cars. Then he had
done a few respraying jobs of his own. He'd
resprayed all the red pillar boxes duck-egg blue,
resprayed the village green purple, and resprayed
the mayor's official black limousine with pink and
white candy stripes. The postman was not amused,
the council gardeners were not amused, and the
mayor was furious. And now all of them had

joined in to increase the reward for the capture of Elf Azard.

'This is your last chance to get that reward, Fat Witch,' said Chief Witch. 'The mayor's last words on the phone were that if we don't capture Elf Azard ourselves he'll call in the C.I.D.'

'The Criminal Investigation Department?' asked Fat Witch.

'No, the "Constables in Disguise" brigade.'

'Oh, not that lot,' said Fat Witch. 'They never solve anything. Last time they were here looking for that cat burglar, they dressed up as old ladies and ate up all the cream cakes in Mrs Copper's cake shop. They didn't fool anyone. Everyone knew who they were, clumping around in their great heavy boots and knitted stockings. One of them even had a beard and a black moustache. And they didn't catch the cat burglar. He let the cats that he had stolen go free and they all went home to their owners, none the worse.'

'Well, it's up to you, Fat Witch. One last chance to catch Elf Azard or in comes the C.I.D. and out goes your chance of getting the reward and the vroomstick.'

Fat Witch left Chief Witch's office, deep in thought. How was she going to catch Elf Azard? He'd been too clever for her so far. She walked down the village street, past the postman repainting the pillar boxes, past the gardeners hosing down the grass, and came to the garage where Big Al himself, in a suit of grey overalls, was respraying the mayor's official car.

'This car's had more coats than a millionaire,' he said to Fat Witch as she stopped to watch. 'And I can still see the candy stripes. But what are you

doing here? I thought you were hot on the trail of
Elf Azard?'

'So did I,' said Fat Witch sadly.

'Well, luckily he didn't think of respraying the
vroomstick, but I'm sorry to have to tell you that
I've had another inquiry about the vroomstick. A
customer who saw my ad in the paper is interested
in buying it.'

Fat Witch's ears shot up. 'Another witch?'

'Has to be, hasn't it?' said Big Al. 'Only witches
get a licence for these things.'

'Who is it?' asked Fat Witch. 'Anybody I know?'

'Might be,' said Big Al.

'Well, it can't be Chief Witch, or she'd have

said,' said Fat Witch. 'And it can't be Granny Witch because she lost her licence for drinking too much Witch's special brew last Hallowe'en. Tall Witch is afraid of heights and travels by scooter, and Small Witch hasn't passed her driving test yet. So it must be . . . oh, no . . .' She looked at Big Al who grinned and nodded his head.

'Not Slinky Witch?' she said.

'Certainly is,' said Big Al. 'She came in yesterday. Said she was looking for a new model to

compliment her image. Something sleek and slinky like herself.'

Fat Witch's heart sank. Slinky Witch, the most attractive, most beautiful, slimmest witch in the whole country, and now she wanted the vroomstick as well.

'But you can't sell the vroomstick to Slinky Witch,' said Fat Witch. 'She hasn't got a nice personality. You can't sell that lovely vroomstick to someone who's not a nice person. She won't look after it, you know. She'll leave it out in the rain. She'll run it into the air.'

Fat Witch knew Big Al's weakness. He worried about the transport he sold. He liked all his models to go to good homes.

Then Fat Witch played her last card. She knew if there was one thing Big Al couldn't stand it was people who left sticky sweetie papers stuck to his models. Unfortunately Slinky Witch didn't eat sweets or cakes or biscuits. It was enough to make you sick. But Fat Witch had had a brainwave. 'Slinky Witch will leave,' she said, 'her sugarless chewing gum parked in amongst the bristles.'

That did it. Big Al turned white at the very thought. 'All right, Fat Witch,' he said. 'You win. One more day. I'll hold the vroomstick for one more day. But that's all you've got to catch Elf Azard and claim the reward. Otherwise the vroomstick goes to Slinky Witch. I've got a business to run. I can't say fairer than that.'

'Thanks, Big Al. You're a pal,' said Fat Witch, and she skipped home, smiling. Though why, she wasn't sure, for she still hadn't thought of a way to catch Elf Azard and she only had twenty-four hours left.

CHAPTER SEVEN
Slinky Witch Gets Nasty

Joe King was having a lovely dream. He dreamt that he and Fat Witch were on a cruise ship. The big liner sailed on a glass-like ocean, and the sun shone from a perfect sky. Joe King was lying in the shade of Fat Witch who was wearing her rent-a-tent bikini in a slimming shade of camouflage. Her pointed hat sported a little flag to show that they were on holiday. Joe King had just rolled over and spotted the ship's cat, Miss Felicity Feline, and was just strolling over to have a word with her when 'OWWWWWCHCH'. Fat Witch arrived home and trod on his tail which he had carelessly left lying out on the carpet while the rest of him was safely asleep under a chair.

'Why can't you look where you're putting your great fat feet, Fat Witch?' he yowled.

'I have very dainty feet, actually,' sniffed Fat

Witch. 'Many slightly bigger than average size people do, you know, if you care to look closely. Anyway why don't you tuck your tail away tidily like other cats do? It's always where it shouldn't be.'

'It's always stuck on to the end of me, and that's where it should be,' muttered Joe King.

'In any case,' said Fat Witch, 'I'm sure my feet are getting smaller. It must be all this walking. They'll be worn away soon.'

'Then perhaps you should try walking on your b . . .'

'What?'

'Nothing. Any luck with Chief Witch and the Elf Azard problem?'

'Not really,' said Fat Witch and wandered into

the kitchen.

She put on the kettle which didn't suit her so she made a cup of tea instead and told Joe King all that had happened.

Joe King blew out his cheeks. 'Only twenty-four hours. Not long, Fat Witch. Not long at all. Why that's only one thousand four hundred and forty minutes or eighty-six thousand and four hundred seconds or, put another way, just one day.'

'Thanks, Joe King,' said Fat Witch. 'You're a great comfort to me.'

'I do my best,' said Joe King.

Then they both sat in glum silence over their cups of tea, thinking about the problem.

'I don't suppose . . . ?' said Fat Witch.

'Wouldn't work,' said Joe King, reading her thoughts. 'What about . . . ?'

'No chance,' said Fat Witch, reading his.

'Forget it,' they both said together, reading each others thoughts.

They sighed. Loudly. In unison.

Just then there was a loud popping noise, some eye-watering smoke, and Slinky Witch stood skinnily in front of them.

'I popped in to see you,' she said, 'because I went into the garage yesterday to buy that beautiful vroomstick which is so right for ME, and I heard that WHEN you've caught Elf Azard, you're going to claim the reward and buy the vroomstick for yourself.'

'That's right,' said Fat Witch.

'You, on a vroomstick,' sneered Slinky Witch. 'Don't make me laugh.'

'Why, do your bones rattle and give you a fright?' asked Joe King.

Slinky Witch gave him such a look that a lump of fur on the top of his head fell out.

'Shush, Joe King,' said Fat Witch. 'I'll deal with this. I saw the vroomstick first, Slinky Witch. Big Al's keeping it for me, and I'm going to buy it tomorrow.'

Slinky Witch gave a laugh that curdled the milk in their tea.

'Not if I've got anything to do with it.'

'What have you got to with it, Slinky Witch? Elf Azard is spoiling this place for everybody with his dirty tricks. Surely you want to see him get caught.'

But Slinky Witch didn't answer. With another milk-curdling laugh and a loud pop, she was gone.

'Now I know why Elf Azard has been so clever,' said Fat Witch. 'I bet he's had Slinky Witch to help him. I knew she wasn't a nice person, but that makes it harder than ever to catch him because Slinky Witch is really clever.'

Fat Witch's shoulders rounded in despair.

'Cheer up, Fat Witch,' said Joe King. 'You've still got me to help you.'

Fat Witch stroked the bald spot Slinky Witch had caused.

'I know, Joe King. You've always managed to cheer me up when things looked black.'

'Do you remember,' said Joe King, 'that time at your birthday when the candles set your birthday cake on fire and we had to call the fire brigade? I made you another birthday cake.'

'I remember. A spaghetti and chips birthday cake. It was very unusual.'

'Do you remember,' Joe King continued, 'that winter it was so cold you came home from

71

shopping, frozen on to your broomstick? I got you unstuck.'

'I remember. You threw a bucket of warm water over me. I didn't mind the warm water but it was a pity you let go of the bucket. Still, the bruises soon faded.'

'Do you remember that other time when you decided to have a party and . . . ?'

'That's it,' cried Fat Witch, jumping up and knocking Joe King over. 'A party. Tonight we'll have a party. We'll invite everybody in the village. Elf Azard won't be able to resist making mischief at that, and we'll catch him on our very own doorstep.'

CHAPTER EIGHT

Come to a Party

Fat Witch and Joe King got out their party notepaper and sat down to write out the invitations. They wrote:

FAT WITCH AND JOE KING INVITE YOU
TO A WITCH'S COSTUME PARTY
TONIGHT AT THEIR HOUSE
"DUNSPELLIN" AT 7.00 P.M.
LOTS OF EATS AND TREATS.

Then they delivered them to all the people in the village.

'There, that's done,' said Fat Witch. 'Now let's do the shopping and get ready for the party.'

Joe King wasn't quite sure how to dress up as a witch for the party so he just stuck some gold stars on to the bald patch Slinky Witch had left him with and tied a gold ribbon round his tail.

'You look very nice, Joe King,' said Fat Witch. 'How do I look?'

73

Joe King looked at her. She was wearing her same old black dress and pointed hat.

'You look just like yourself, Fat Witch. I thought you were going to be in disguise.'

'I am,' said Fat Witch triumphantly, and she produced a black mask from her pocket. 'No one will recognise me in this, will they?'

She put it on. She looked just like Fat Witch in a black mask.

'No one will know it's you at all,' lied Joe King. He'd forgiven her for standing on his tail, and didn't want to hurt her feelings.

'Now,' said Fat Witch, 'I've got the special custard powder safely under my hat, so I'll be ready for the first sign of Elf Azard. While I'm opening the front door to the guests, you position yourself on the window ledge so that you can keep a lookout for anything suspicious.'

'Like what?' asked Joe King.

'Like Elf Azard dressed as a witch. Remember the fish van trick.'

'But how will I know it's him if he's dressed as a witch?'

'Look at the eyes,' said Fat Witch. 'You can always tell a suspicious character by his eyes.'

'I see,' said Joe King, lying again. 'Suspicious eyes.'

Then the party began.

The mayor was the first to arrive, dressed in an old black dressing-gown and a bowler hat.

'I'm sorry the costume's not up to much, Fat Witch,' he said. 'But it was the best I could do at such short notice. Though somewhere at the back of my mind I seem to remember having a donkey outfit. Still that wouldn't have done for this party, would it? Tell me, did you guess it was me?'

'Only by your gold chain peeking out from your collar, Mr Mayor,' said Fat Witch.

Joe King rolled his eyes heavenwards. 'Telling lies must be catching,' he thought.

Tall Witch and Small Witch came together. They had changed frocks so that Tall Witch's knobbly knees were showing and Small Witch kept walking up the inside of her dress and falling over. But they giggled a lot and made everybody laugh.

Granny Witch giggled a lot too. She had brought with her a special punch-bowl. The golden liquid in it looked delicious, but whenever anyone reached in to get a glass of it, a large boxing glove shot out of the middle and punched them on the nose. That made Granny Witch giggle even more. She was the only one who could safely take a drink.

Soon 'Dunspellin' was overflowing with all the witches and the other people from the village. They were laughing and chatting and having a good time. Then, all of a sudden, there was a cry and a yell.

'I've caught him. I've caught him,' yelled Joe King, clinging round the ankle of a witch dressed all in silver. 'I've caught Elf Azard. Just look at him. Have you ever seen such suspicious looking eyes?'

'Fat Witch,' said the witch dressed in silver, 'kindly get this creature off me before I turn him into something really nasty like two-week-old fish paste.'

'Let go. Let go, Joe King,' shouted Fat Witch. 'That's not who you think it is.'

He let go, and sat back.

'Thank you,' said Chief Witch. 'Suspicious eyes, indeed. I'm wearing my new Silvaglit eye-shadow. The cat must be mad.' And she swept in past Fat Witch and joined in the frantic disco dancing.

'Keep a lookout and behave yourself, Joe King,' muttered Fat Witch. 'I'm going into the kitchen to get the food.'

When she opened the door to the kitchen, however, she found Slinky Witch in there, hovering by the table.

'Hello, Slinky Witch,' she said. 'I didn't see you come in the front door.'

'Oh, I just popped straight in here to see if I could give you a hand with the eats,' purred Slinky Witch. 'To make up for being rather nasty earlier on. I was just so disappointed about the vroomstick, that's all. I really do apologise. But, everything looks so delicious, Fat Witch. Too nice to eat, really. Here, let me help you carry everything in.'

And she was so pleasant and friendly that Fat Witch began to think that her suspicions about her must have been wrong. Slinky Witch smiled and fussed round the table with her back to Fat Witch, so that Fat Witch didn't see her adding a pinch of some purple powder to the puddings and pies.

Cheerfully, Fat Witch carried in the food. 'Come and get it, everybody,' she called.

Everyone crowded round and started biting into the food.

'Aargh, ugh, ow, ow,' they all shouted. 'We've been poisoned.'

The mayor clutched at his throat and purple smoke came out of his ears. Chief Witch's eye-shadow turned liquid and ran in silver trickles

down her cheeks, and Mr Wong shook his head and thought British cooking was truly terrible. Everyone coughed and spluttered.

Everyone, that is, except Slinky Witch who hadn't touched a morsel. She smiled nastily.

'Oh, you poor things,' she said. 'I never eat anything Fat Witch has made. You know, for all she's so fat, she's really not much of a cook.'

'Don't worry, Fat Witch,' said Joe King appearing at her side. 'The extra lemonade that you ordered has just been delivered. I've given everyone a drink to wash away the horrible taste. They'll be all right in a moment.'

'Extra lemonade,' said Fat Witch. 'But we're having orange squash. I didn't order extra lemonade. Oh, no, look everyone's turning green now. There must be something ghastly in the lemonade too.'

Then she saw a man standing in the corner with an empty lemonade crate in his hand. He was wearing a mask and a long black witch's cloak, but peeping out from the bottom of the cloak was a pair of green boots. And the masked stranger was laughing fit to burst. Fat Witch knew who he was. With a flying leap she was on him. She was so angry, she forgot all about the special custard powder. She forgot all about the party. She forgot all about Granny Witch's punch-bowl as she brought Elf Azard down in a special Fat Witch tackle. Elf Azard gave a loud yell as his head sloshed into the punch-bowl, and a louder yell when Granny Witch's boxing glove came out and socked him on the nose.

Meanwhile, Joe King, realising what was happening had slipped over beside Slinky Witch

and, in the commotion, had tied her leg to the table with the gold ribbon from his tail.

'She won't find it so easy to pop off anywhere with a table tied to her leg,' he muttered.

By now, Elf Azard was well and truly caught. Fat Witch held him by one arm, the mayor by the other while Granny Witch stood guard with her punch-bowl not ten centimetres away from his pointed nose. Elf Azard was going nowhere this time and was confessing everything.

'It was all Slinky Witch's fault,' he said. 'She knew I was angry with Chief Witch for taking away my magic powers, so she promised that if I would help her do nasty things around here to discredit Chief Witch she would give me back my magic powers when she was made Chief Witch instead.'

'I thought as much,' muttered Chief Witch, who

had fixed Slinky Witch with a look that froze her to the spot. 'I've had my suspicions about Slinky Witch for some time, but I couldn't prove anything. She was very clever.'

'It was Slinky Witch's idea to steal the cats a while back, too,' went on Elf Azard. 'I was the cat burglar. I stole them all from the Fishmonger's

yard where they'd gathered when he threw out a load of old fish heads.'

'You didn't get me,' smirked Joe King, who sniffed and looked superior.

'No,' said Chief Witch. 'And thanks to you and Fat Witch, we've uncovered the real villain. I had racked my brains trying to think of ways to make Slinky Witch break cover and Fat Witch wanting to buy the vroomstick gave me the chance I was looking for. I knew Slinky Witch wouldn't be able to bear the thought of someone else having a vroomstick like that. Well done, Fat Witch.'

Elf Azard and Slinky Witch were marched away by Constable Goggin and Chief Witch. There would be no escaping this time. Everyone congratulated Fat Witch and Joe King. And Mr Wong, who had closed his takeaway because of the party, opened it up again and gave everyone a really good feed to celebrate.

'Thanks to you,' they all said to Fat Witch, 'we don't need to worry about that pair messing everything up around here any more.'

'And thanks to Chief Witch and all the others,' said Fat Witch, 'I can replace my old broomstick with the new vroomstick which I shall be very careful with. No carrying too much shopping ever again. Though, funnily enough, once you get used

to this walking business it's really quite good fun. What do you think, Joe King? Should we forget about the vroomstick and just walk everywhere instead?'

'You must be joking,' said Joe King.

'I think we've done that joke already,' laughed Fat Witch.

EAST LOTHIAN
DISTRICT LIBRARY

Also by Margaret Ryan

QUEEN BEA THE CHAMPION

Queen Bea is thrilled to bits when the royal guardsmen organise an 'It's a Knockout competition' to be held in the palace gardens. She begins practising immediately, and with the help of her friends, Queen Aixalot, Princess Proper and King Cornerswell, she guarantees that the competition will be a great success. Even though the events are rather unusual . . .

Margaret Ryan

QUEEN BEA ON HOLIDAY

Queen Bea is so excited at the prospect of going on holiday that she books up the whole of Sunsea Holiday Camp so that everyone in the palace can go. She packs her bags immediately, and accompanied by her friends, Queen Aixalot, Princess Proper and King Cornerswell, she sets out for the adventure holiday of a lifetime.

Margaret Ryan

KING TUBBITUM AND
THE LITTLE COOK

"Send for the little cook!" cries King Tubbitum whenever
anything goes wrong at the palace. And whether the
problem is a throne that's too tight, a princess who can't
get to sleep, or a cross and hungry dragon, the little cook
puts everything right with a mixture of common sense
and good cooking.

Margaret Ryan

KING TUBBITUM AT THE FAIR

King Tubbitum loves food more than anything else. He eats from dawn to dusk. He's so fat that none of his royal robes fit him any more. Something must be done. Perhaps the arrival of the travelling fair will take his mind off food? Oh no! The Fat Lady of the fair wants the King to come for tea . . .

Margaret Ryan

KING TUBBITUM AND THE GREAT SPRING CLEAN

King Tubbitum has let the Royal Palace get very untidy.
And when his friends, King Greenbean, King Poshnosh,
Queen Slenderella and Queen Fussiface come to tea they
are horrified by the mess and make him promise to tidy it
up. Which is just what he does. King Tubbitum plans a
bumper party to celebrate . . . but will he be able to keep
the Palace clean?

Anne Fine

A SUDDEN PUFF OF GLITTERING SMOKE

"Not G-e-n-i-e! J-e-a-n-i-e!"
The creature shrugged. "One little mistake," he said.
"Even a genie gets rusty after five hundred years stuck in a ring."

The disgruntled genie who appears on her desk seems to be the answer to Jeanie's problems – whatever she wishes, he will command. But Jeanie quickly discovers that she and her genie have very different views of the world.

A Sudden Puff of Glittering Smoke is the first part in Anne Fine's trilogy about a genie; followed by *A Sudden Swirl of Icy Wind*, the trilogy is concluded in *A Sudden Glow of Gold*.

Anne Fine is the winner of the Smarties Award (for *Bill's New Frock*) and the Carnegie Medal.

Andrew Matthews

WICKEDOZ

A witch's cat by trade and a wily cat by nature, Wickedoz
finds himself without a witch so sets out in search of fame
and fortune. But will Gerald Fitzgerald-Fitzgerald the
Third help him find what he seeks, and will the wicked
Mistress Moonwater make it possible . . .?

Andrew Matthews

MISTRESS MOONWATER

Mistress Moonwater, the most chronic chrone in the chronicle, is living in semi-retirement in Dunspellin Castle. Meanwhile, in Heartland, a fairy tale is in the making. Princess Cheryl, the beloved and nearly beautiful, is to marry Prince Craig of Constantia, the quite clever prince. Or is she?

Egged on by Lord Cringe of Nobbly Wallop, Mistress Moonwater has other ideas . . .

A Selected List of Fiction from Mammoth

While every effort is made to keep prices low, it is sometimes necessary to increase prices at short notice. Mammoth Books reserves the right to show new retail prices on covers which may differ from those previously advertised in the text or elsewhere.

The prices shown below were correct at the time of going to press.

☐ 7497 0366 0	**Dilly the Dinosaur**	Tony Bradman	£1.99
☐ 7497 0021 1	**Dilly and the Tiger**	Tony Bradman	£1.99
☐ 7497 0137 4	**Flat Stanley**	Jeff Brown	£1.99
☐ 7497 0048 3	**Friends and Brothers**	Dick King-Smith	£1.99
☐ 7497 0054 8	**My Naughty Little Sister**	Dorothy Edwards	£1.99
☐ 416 86550 X	**Cat Who Wanted to go Home**	Jill Tomlinson	£1.99
☐ 7497 0166 8	**The Witch's Big Toe**	Ralph Wright	£1.99
☐ 7497 0218 4	**Lucy Jane at the Ballet**	Susan Hampshire	£2.25
☐ 416 03212 5	**I Don't Want To!**	Bel Mooney	£1.99
☐ 7497 0030 0	**I Can't Find It!**	Bel Mooney	£1.99
☐ 7497 0032 7	**The Bear Who Stood on His Head**	W. J. Corbett	£1.99
☐ 416 10362 6	**Owl and Billy**	Martin Waddell	£1.75
☐ 416 13822 5	**It's Abigail Again**	Moira Miller	£1.75
☐ 7497 0031 9	**King Tubbitum and the Little Cook**	Margaret Ryan	£1.99
☐ 7497 0041 6	**The Quiet Pirate**	Andrew Matthews	£1.99
☐ 7497 0064 5	**Grump and the Hairy Mammoth**	Derek Sampson	£1.99

All these books are available at your bookshop or newsagent, or can be ordered direct from the publisher. Just tick the titles you want and fill in the form below.

Mandarin Paperbacks, Cash Sales Department, PO Box 11, Falmouth, Cornwall TR10 9EN.

Please send cheque or postal order, no currency, for purchase price quoted and allow the following for postage and packing:

UK 80p for the first book, 20p for each additional book ordered to a maximum charge of £2.00.

BFPO 80p for the first book, 20p for each additional book.

Overseas including Eire £1.50 for the first book, £1.00 for the second and 30p for each additional book thereafter.

NAME (Block letters) ....

ADDRESS ....

....

....